*For Cari~
with my ever
and love over
9 months.
Namaste Vanessa*

Soul Kissing

Soul Kissing

A collection of playful Poetry and Prose

*'Let me kiss your soul
With the thoughts of my heart'*

Michelle Schaper

Copyright © 2016 by Michelle Schaper.

ISBN:	Softcover	978-1-5245-1682-6
	eBook	978-1-5245-1681-9

All rights reserved. No part of this book may be reproduced or transmitted in any form or by any means, electronic or mechanical, including photocopying, recording, or by any information storage and retrieval system, without permission in writing from the copyright owner.

This is a work of fiction. Names, characters, places and incidents either are the product of the author's imagination or are used fictitiously, and any resemblance to any actual persons, living or dead, events, or locales is entirely coincidental.

Any people depicted in stock imagery provided by Thinkstock are models, and such images are being used for illustrative purposes only.
Certain stock imagery © Thinkstock.

Print information available on the last page.

Rev. date: 08/26/2016

To order additional copies of this book, contact:
Xlibris
1-800-455-039
www.Xlibris.com.au
Orders@Xlibris.com.au
723473

Contents

Soul Kissing 1
Rhetorically Persuaded 2
My Memory Tree 4
Free Spirit 6
Serenity and Chaos 7
The Jewel Inside A Dream 9
Chantilly Dreams 10
Tomorrow's Wings 12
Pieces of Dreams 13
The Essence of A Woman 14
I Made A Home Out of The Walls I Built Around My Heart 15
Falling Stars - The Tears of A Goddess 17
Forever A Memory 18
The Muse 19
Nirvana 20
Tingles In My Feelings 21
Hope In My Heart 22
Seasons of Love 23
Imprints 24
My Song 25
Wild Love 26
Grounding 27
Whispers of Truth 28
Adornment 29
Timeless Love 30
Gentle Strength 31
Breathless 32
Fallen 33
Droplets of Love 34

Shimmer	35
Unbroken	36
Poetic Kisses	37
Yin & Yang	38
Show Her Your Genius	39
Pieces of My Heart	40
Heavenly Sin	41
True Beauty Comes From The Heart	42
Yesterday's Fragility Won't End Today's Possibility	43
Salt of The Soul	44
Heavens Sword	45
If You Were The Moon	46
Dream Catcher	47
My Immortal	48
Create Your Own Sunshine	49
Cascading Passion	50
Tiny Soldiers	51
Stardust	52
Balancing Dualism	53
Hungry Heart	54
Hurricane Heart	55
The Magic of Children	56
Lunar Soul	57
Scars	58
Heart Song	59
The Beauty You See In Me Is A Reflection of What's Beautiful In You	60
Redefining Romance	61
Rainbows	62
Gypsy Soul	63
Happily Ever After	64
Soul Mate	65
SoulFire	66
Wings of A Storm	67

Sensitive Souls	68
Butterflies	69
Shadow Keeper	70
Kissing Cannibals	71
Dance	72
Permanent Daylight	73
Sea of Hopes & Dreams	74
Sleepless Memories	75
Diamonds & Pearls	76
Fairytale Charm	77
Her Own Kind of Divinity	78
She Is You	79
Rhythm of Life	80
Realm of Romance	81
Majestic Grace	82
Footprints	83
Silken Threads	84
Rare Gem	85
Alpha	86
Pokerface	87
Crown	88
Sea of Love	89
Empathy	90
Make Love To My Mind	91
Sips of Stars	92
Forget-Me-Not	93
Inner Child	94
Stain	95
Independent Woman	96
Infinite Potential	97
Perpetual Princess	98
FireStone	99
Whiskey Angels with Wings of Ink	100

Dedication

For Chelsea and Tiana

~ Soul Kissing ~

Sometimes she is the poet
Always she is the poem

However wild her heart is
Wherever she may roam

She doesn't love with just her eyes
That's not what makes her whole

So place your lips upon her heart
And kiss her gentle soul

*'To her every word was like a little kiss
Each blank page a lost soul
And every time she would write
She was simply Soul Kissing'*

~ Rhetorically Persuaded ~

When the Mistress of metaphors gives you a glimpse of her mind
Whispering wings of enchantment you'll be sure to find
Flying through dreamscapes, wandering all through the night, kissing stars while you follow her glittering light
Sometimes her glow dims, to a soft opaque shine, when shadows stop by to kiss this soul of mine
A heart so fragile can be too heavy to bear, so she'll take you on a magical ride, through the darkness dwelling there
She can dress up her memories of past pain or death, make your soul sigh, until you lose your breath
Turning nightmares into dreams that you'll wish for at night, she believes we all need some darkness to truly see light
Just like Yin needs Yang, we all balance somehow, it just flows, sometimes aesthetically, from the lips of a Princess of Prose
When they come together, this blending of words, we find beauty in what's broken, music from the song-less birds
This Princess shows her sultry style with an elegant attitude full of dynamic emotions, she's sensually connected, often shrewd
She'll take you on a journey of naughty and nice
Teasing edges of ecstasy, all the way to paradise
Her words painting pictures with sensations in part bringing goosebumps, tears, and warmth to your heart

So the Mistress of Metaphors and the Princess of Prose
would like to take you to a romantic realm, where not everyone goes
Knowing the magic is already there, they just like to enhance it, for you all to share

If you choose to read her
One page at a time
Let each piece of her story
captivate your mind
With rhetoric persuasion
and whispering dreams
She'll turn all ordinary
Into more than it seems
So open your heart
to enhance all you'll see
and prepare to embark
on a new level
of fantasy'

~ My Memory Tree ~

I have known darkness
It's shown itself to me at the hands of others
Then crawled inside my mind to stay

But when the shadows rear themselves
My cognisance has learnt to create a new path
And tell the gloominess 'no, not today'

This road leads to a forest of enchantment
Changing my perception
To show my intellect a different quality

Here I'll find ethereal beauty
Never a shadow of a doubt
Not one bit of tenebrosity

These whispering woods breathe my name
Permeating stories to be told
Throughout the fortresses of glorious trees

One stands out proud from the others
Like a tall flowering tower
It's the tree of all my happy memories

Moments of joy and pleasure
Imbedded in woody essence
So many timeless deep twisting roots

Abundant branches sprouting
With blossom-filled twigs extended
Each flower holding more florets with new tiny shoots

Every petal represents a favourite moment
Each new shoot perhaps a moment yet to come
The little moments are the things in life I like the most

I often visit my forest of enchantment
Re-visit my favourite moments I've collected
Because my future is uncertain
And my past is just a ghost

'All my favourite moments shine like little stars that glow and spark
My happy memories each light up to guide me through times of dark'

~ Free Spirit ~

She has the soul of a gypsy, she's messy and wild,
She's full of wonder and thinks like a child.
She is a mosaic, pieces of light,
She's the moon and the stars shining so bright.
She's the breath of fresh air that whispers in your ear,
She is always with you, even when she's not near.
She is all of the sky and the wings of the birds,
She's poetry, lyrics, music and words.
She's the eye of the tiger, the howl of the wolf,
She is a paradox, a metaphor, but always the truth.
She is caged by her thoughts,
But she's eternally free,
She's nothing, she's everything
I think she is me ...

'She is a fireball of passion wrapped up in a gentle heart'

~ Serenity and Chaos ~

You are a rock of strength
Whenever I need grounding
I am an ocean
For only you to drown in

Personified peace
Calmness epitomised
Make me feel at ease
Somewhat mystified

Standing solid through a storm
Crashing through depths of the deepest ocean
While I surf the turbulent waves
Of every known emotion

I'm filled with sensibilities
Using my every sense
You paint my world with tranquility
If I become too intense

You are the only one
Who's ever seemed to know
How to paradox my sensitivities
Make my heart beat fast and slow

I see intangibles when I look into your eyes
That I will never reach for
Yet they have me realise

I will be receptive
To let your intangibilities touch me
So I can cherish all our moments shared
However few they'll be

*'I will love completely and passionately
but never possessively'*

~ The Jewel Inside A Dream ~

There aren't any pennies in my pocket
around my neck's no shiny locket
but I mostly wear a smile upon my lips

My shoes and clothes aren't fancy
I don't wear silken panties
But you'll find a sensual swing within my hips

And though I don't own precious stones
my skin won't be fragranced by expensive colognes
my hands will be warm for you to hold

My only jewels sparkle in my eyes
or are found between my thighs
but my most valued asset is by far my heart of gold

'She is sensually connected
full of dynamic emotions
playful, with an unconscious coquetry
You'll see she has a heart of pure gold
Firestone fills her soul
And her mind produces
pearls of poetry'

~ Chantilly Dreams ~

Her skin may be soft
light as a feather
But her heart is bound
encased by tough leather
Make sure that you
do not 'judge a book'
She'll have you hypnotised
with only one look
Once you've been allured
by her elegant charm
It will be too late
to raise any alarm
For when you enter
her inextricable maze
You'll be under her spell,
left in an enchanted daze
It's here you'll realise
the strength of her mind
you'll be trapped in
an intricate labyrinthine
Where Chantilly dreams
are stitched, and filigree thoughts
are weaved delicately
into a magic of sorts

Her wild heart
may be hardened
stained many moons ago
Though if she lets you in
through the raw skin
you'll come to know
The secret her soul keeps
gives her the power to embrace
every entanglement thrown her way
She is ... Leather and Lace

'Threads of insecurity sewn to her skin at the hands of others unravelled long ago
Replaced by silken ribbons of love she has found within herself'

Michelle Schaper

~ Tomorrow's Wings ~

Each time she opened her eyes
to a brand new day
The sunshine smiled upon her
to light the way
Yesterday's story now hiding
secrets to be told
Today dusts off her wings
allowing them to unfold
She opens her heart
as she opens her eyes
Spreading her wings
she looks up to the skies
She'll fly through today
finding new ways to cope
Because her soul's seen tomorrow
through visions of hope

*'Each new day brings a dawn of innocence
for yesterday is sleeping and tomorrow isn't promised'*

~ Pieces of Dreams ~

I always
close my eyes
to feel the things
my heart can see
The wonder
of it all
The world
and its true beauty
And sometimes
when dreams appear
in little pieces
not quite whole
My heart
will find you there
sleeping
inside my soul ...

'Whisper me a dream and I'll kiss you a story'

~ The Essence of A Woman ~

She took integrity and kindness
And mixed it with some grace
Threw in a bit of wildness
And beauty for her face
She added some compassion
And a touch of elegance
Along with empathy and passion
Strength and intelligence
The best part kept deep inside
Her soul shining from within
Sense and sensitivity
Then wrapped it all up
with her skin

'If you get close enough to look into her eyes
You'll see they're just the right shade of poetry'

~ I Made A Home Out of The Walls I Built Around My Heart ~

Sometimes I get lost
Deep inside of my own heart
So many little chambers
With winding paths to every part
One room is full of art, tattooed within there
Memories of all
Who've shown me that they care
Pictures on the walls
Of familiar faces
A treasure trove of love
Maps of my favourite places
One section is quite dark
That door is opened rarely
The walls stained with ugly scars
That left me breathing barely
And buried in the corners
Of the dark room on the floor
Piles of broken arrows
Cupid attempts from long before
One of my most cherished spaces

Deep in this heart of mine
Where you kiss me up against the walls
Time after time
Passion burns brightly here
Running rampant like wildfire
Music and lyrics making my heart beat
To a rhythm of desire
Sometimes my walls tower high
Pushing so many away
But this is my humble home
No matter where in life I stay

*'Sometimes I get the feeling
there's nowhere I could belong
Until I place my hand upon my chest
And let my heartbeat bring me home'*

~ Falling Stars -
The Tears of A Goddess ~

There were oceans
in her gentle heart
Rolling waves
chased petal dreams
Sometimes crashing
through her patchwork soul
fraying all the seams
Stormy seas
behind wild eyes
A fragile heart
that leaks
But what a beautiful
chaotic world
Collapsed
upon her cheeks

*'The tears of a goddess drop like ethereal pearls
upon cheeks that used to smile
And the shooting stars which once lit up her eyes
have all fallen'*

~ Forever A Memory ~

You'll try not to think of me
As i linger on your skin
You'll start to ache inside
As I haunt you from within
My taste will burn like wildfire
Throughout your memory
And in the ashes left behind
You will be craving me

*'She was like a fine Whiskey
you'd feel honoured to taste
One sip of her warmth
will leave a burn
in your hearts place'*

~ The Muse ~

She is
that tender touch
on the back
of your neck
from caressing fingertips

She is
primitive art
admired from afar
Just the right shade
of ruby lips

She is
the gentle breeze
who will know
when to lift
your tired, tattered wings

She is
a little bird
who'll guide your voice
inspiring all
when she sings

'Her whole body throbs with energy
Like a heart beating, burst from an open chest
With a force that could break bones
She moves poetically, a writers dream.
Dripping with ink, gliding straight off of a page
She is a sonnet, a timeless story
Unstained by reality'

~ Nirvana ~

If Paradise exists
I don't think it is a place
It's something else
Like a feeling or a taste
It could be that moment
when you make a wish
or the gentle eyelash stroke
of a butterfly kiss
I don't believe It could be
of anyones creation
It's deep inside your soul
in every beautiful sensation

*'I heard the wind whisper
and the earth sigh
It made my soul smile
as I walked by'*

~ Tingles In My Feelings ~

You see my soul is sensitive
Not everybody understands
What it's like to feel so much
Have things I touch burn my hands
I wonder if they saw how visually
Just what emotions do to me
I suspect many would resonate
If sensations felt, they all could see
When I see or hear something beautiful
And goosebumps dance upon my skin
It would look like fragmented ice
Shattering from within
Shivers come in waves
All throughout the day
As if an ocean lives inside of me
Sometimes crashing on my bay
When I'm outside for just a while
Sensations are profound
Sensibilities are amplified
Especially scent and sound
Covering my skin
You'd see little sun shaped lips
The warmth of the sunshine
Feels like every inch of me
Is given a gentle kiss
And tears, tears are frequent visitors
They make kaleidoscopes in my eyes
With tiny pins and needles
Stinging, while each cheek is baptised

'Sometimes I can feel vibrations between all the tiny spaces between my bones, it's like my whole body is breathing while I'm drowning in depths of emotions.'

~ Hope In My Heart ~

I close my eyes to feel the breeze
dance upon my skin

The sensation takes me far away
and warms me from within

I'm floating to somewhere
hidden deep behind my eyes

Some place I've been before

Where dreams
have wings like butterflies

The word 'hope' is
intricately carved into a door

Turning the handle
to step inside I find wishes
Fluttering through
every part

Then I realise
where I've travelled to ….

The hope inside my heart

*'When your heart is ready
your wings will carry you upon
a gentle breeze of hope'*

~ Seasons of Love ~

Her smile is like a portrait of Summer
She has skin of silk, Winter-light
All the stars made a home in her eyes
Where they sparkle and twinkle so bright
There's Spring in her step when she walks
With a rhythm that imitates rain
She wears a dress sewn out of Autumn
And a mask to hide all her pain

*'If you could see yourself like others do
You'd wish you were as beautiful as You'*

~ Imprints ~

I know you're out there somewhere
I heard my heart telling my soul
Your kisses imprinted upon my skin
Many moons ago

Lovers come and lovers go
But none of them are you
They say and do all the right things
They believe their love is true

Whether this lifetime or the next
I know we'll meet again
I'll keep the aching in my bones
For all the while 'till then

I know you're out there somewhere
I heard the moon whisper to the sea
You made an imprint in my soul
The others only touch me

'The moment my soul recognised yours
My heart shivered
There's been a fever in my bones since'

~ My Song ~

I have a heart made of patchwork
And a hand-me-down soul
There's a burn in my bones
My eyes are made of charcoal
There's ink in my veins
And love in my blood
I'm all the flames in a fire
I am the depth of a flood
Inside my mind
Plays an instinctual melody
They'll all dance along
To this song that is me

'Sense the fire deep within your soul, feel the flames of passion burn you as they lick.
Forget everything that you've been told, let the noise inside your head become sweet music.'

~ Wild Love ~

His love
resembled
a night sky
encapsulating her
within a beautiful
darkness
Enveloping her
with an endless
warmth
like a moonlit glow
The stars
in his eyes
hunted her down
but he fell prey
to the wild
in her heart

*"The wild in her heart
left footprints in his soul"*

~ Grounding ~

She needs
the warmth of the sun
Or the glistening
of rain
The moon and stars
when the day is done
and soft pillows
where she's lain
The leaves and the trees
The earth below her feet
Her skin to feel
the breeze
and music, oh so sweet
All these will calm
her mind
and stop her thoughts
from running wild
Smell flowers one at a time
And view the world
just like a child

'Always allow yourself to feel the wonder of everything, whether it be a song or a raindrop. Never let others take away your tenderness because of their own fears. By responding to emotional influences, you will become aesthetic yourself.
True beauty lies within your sensibilities.'

~ Whispers of Truth ~

Somewhere deep inside my heart
Sits my little whisper of truth
She filters all my dreams
Keeps the memories of my youth

Reminding me sometimes
When my mind forgets to know
Of which path I should choose
To let my soul heal and grow

She tenders the fruit of my love there
In passionate colours and shades
Nurturing my inner self
Ensuring that it never fades

Sometimes when I'm feeling sad
She'll take some time to rest
In preparation of new times ahead
Moments my heart will find the best

So my whispering little nymph
Watches over me
when shadows of the heart begin to creep
She is my guiding light who knows just how to weave
the secrets that I keep

'Who's there peeking through your dreams, unravelling stitches from your seams?
Maybe it's your inner self who sits in your heart upon a shelf.
Who's enchanted whisperings do you hear, mystical murmurs through your ear? Maybe it's your authenticity, the 'you' in your soul who you're meant to be.'

~ Adornment ~

Her patchwork soul
had been stitched together
by the hands of time
Skin sewn from silken
threads of moonlight
Her eyes were filled
with Starshine
Her heart made of intricately
woven scars
She was a paradoxical
pastiche of primitive art
with graceful interludes
Everything softened
when you looked at her
just like glistening raindrops
blur a rainy day
But if she glanced your way
you'd feel as though
you've been kissed
by a thousand suns
warming your heart
As she takes your breath away

*'She was dressed exquisitely
in only the softness of her skin
The tenderness of her touch,
and the air was fragranced with all of her mysteries'*

~ Timeless Love ~

Tell me where you go
With your Lion's-heart
Dusty soul
Tattoos of your past
etched deep behind your eyes
I don't know where I've been
except inside a dream
Ageless
Timeless
Weightless
Until again
your soul I recognise

*'His soul is stained
with her wild beauty
And his blood
is the colour of her love.'*

~ Gentle Strength ~

Somewhere deep inside of me
Are precious things you'll never see
They make me laugh or cry and sing
Extreme emotions they can bring
Sometimes life is tough
With what it may deal
But I'd never change how much I feel
Strength is the essence of sensitivity
My feelings help to make me 'ME'
When you're struggling to cope but don't feel quite whole
Look to the infinitely precious things within your soul

'She is as pretty as a glowing butterfly, her mind is worlds apart
She's as gentle as a sleepy Sunday
There must be magic in her heart'

~ Breathless ~

Something happens inside all the spaces between my ribs when I'm with you
It might be my lungs expanding and making them tighten or your presence has me feeling breathless and that's where all my breath goes dancing around
It could be the whisper of wings that grow from my heart as each beat fights the urge to fly straight through my chest
Maybe it's not wings growing but arms
Because just like me, my heart wants to wrap itself around you and never let you go

'He had an aura full of warmth
Even in the coldest evening air
He was a warm gentle breeze
Blowing all the stars around'

~ Fallen ~

An angel fell
Went straight to hell
But crawled on out of there
Her wings got singed
The flames changing
The colour of her hair
But what she learnt
From being burnt
Was worth the scars she gained
Sometimes it's in
our favour
To be re-arranged
For if we fall
And have to crawl
Our strength
will only grow
And if we
never tried
How would we ever know?

*'She hasn't always known love and light, she's done her time in hell.
She's just learned how to dance with her demons so well'*

~ Droplets of Love ~

There's silver liquid dripping from our eyelashes
As the thunder rolls and rain pours
But the only thing I know in this moment
Is the taste of your mouth and how my lips belong to yours

*'I hope you get to feel like you've been born inside of a raindrop
And may your lips find a kiss to build a dream on'*

~ Shimmer ~

She always
watched the world
Through glittering eyes
She saw
everything sparkle
Like starry night skies
And sometimes
When her world
Became a little dimmer
That was when she knew
It was her turn
To shimmer

'And when all the glitter fades
There'll still be stardust
In her veins'

~ Unbroken ~

She is wild and messy
Not a strand of hair in place
Within her soul is beauty
That shines outward through her face
She is lilt, moving musically
And mellifluous when her words are spoken
And when she smiles
The world lights up
You'd never tell
She once felt broken

'She has skin of liquid moonlight
Her eyes hold all the stars
Her inner beauty shines so bright
Through the cracks of all her scars'

~ Poetic Kisses ~

There's no ink stains on my fingers
from what I have been writing
My lips spelled out sweet poetry
with kisses on your skin
Your breath upon my body
was my inspiration
your touch created verses
with each feeling and sensation

'Then he kissed me and I felt poetry melt in my mouth'

~ Yin & Yang ~

I've seen invisible words
As they have been spoken
I have touched a flawless heart
That is so very broken
I can hear the sound of silence
In the light that I can't find
I've been lost in the straight and narrow
On the roads that wind
I have been liberated
While my hands were bound
I've hidden secrets in my soul
Where they can be found

*'If we didn't have places of darkness we know
We wouldn't recognise those who shine and glow'*

~ Show Her Your Genius ~

You taste her silken flesh
with your lustful eyes
Yearning for a drip of honey
sticky-sweet between her thighs
But will you dip your tongue
into her vivacious mind
to savour the pure nectar
of cleverness you'll find
Would you caress the curves
of all the letters in her words
fluttering through her cognisance
like poetic little birds
Will your lips kiss her soul
with words of eloquence
Would you run your fingertips
through her intelligence
Bring her to the edge of ecstasy
as you go down on her pearl of wisdom
As she makes love to your mind
with sensual expressions and her rhythm

*'Loving her body is easy
can you whisper caresses
to each velvet fold
of her mind?'*

Michelle Schaper

~ Pieces of My Heart ~

I leave a piece of me
wherever I may go
A smile for a stranger
A hug for those I know
A heartbeat or a few
For the majestic trees
The essence of my scent
Carried by a gentle breeze
A teardrop for the ocean
A dance in the rain
An echo of laughter
A kiss that leaves a lipstick stain
Everything I'm feeling
Reflecting from my face
The giggle in my hips
As I walk away with grace

'When you give a piece of your heart to another
You're not really giving it away
It makes love in the hearts of others
Becoming more beautiful and strong everyday'

~ Heavenly Sin ~

We all know that certain romance
that leaves a chill in the air
and fire in the heart
A dance with the devil
That feels like a little piece of heaven

'His kiss was my best contradiction, brought out the devil in me while feeling like I'd tasted an angel.'

~ True Beauty Comes From The Heart ~

There's an aching
in her bones
fire beneath her skin
Her circle shaped heart
has no end or beginning
Her mouth tastes like love
her soul sounds poetic
And her eyes redefine
all you think is aesthetic

*'There's a soft edge to her sharp side
if you look from deep inside
your own soul
You'll be able to see
the true shape of her heart'*

~ Yesterday's Fragility Won't End Today's Possibility ~

In the stillness
of each precious moment
When echoes
of sleepless memories
are whispered
Perpetual possibilities
shimmer
like a handful
of diamond dust

*'She had a glittering heart of glass
And every time it shattered
You'd see her shining brighter than the last.'*

~ Salt of The Soul ~

Did you try
to stop
the teardrops
from cascading
through her soul?
Or did you
let her drown there
within the stories
that they told?

'Teardrops come from the ocean of your heart, they are the salt of your soul'

~ Heavens Sword ~

The wind pierced through her
body like a heavens sword
as another lonely winters night came
She held her head high to feel the sweet embrace
of the cold air
then wrapped a blanket of memories around herself
to warm her frozen heart

*'There is a lost soul floating through
a ghostown heart called me
I think she is just searching for
the girl I used to be'*

~ If You Were The Moon ~

If you were the moon
I would be the sky
But you'd be gone too soon
I'd be left high and dry

If you were the ocean
I would be the shore
But then there'd be low tide
And I'd be left wanting more

So I won't be the sky
And you won't be the sea
The best thing to be is you
And I'll be here being me

*'The moonlight whispers memories to me
Of another time and place maybe
Where once upon another life
I was yours and you were mine'*

~ Dream Catcher ~

I will be the promise
you can't keep
As you lay down
to go to sleep
I'll be in your mind
The deepest, darkest bit
To catch your bad dreams
Before you can feel it

'His heartbeat is my lullaby
Loving me to sleep with each breath and sigh'

~ My Immortal ~

The moon is my immortal
my perpetual peace maker
and endless sanctity

In the nights of light
I don't hear whispers in the dark
only shadow tales

Silent ghosts become my phantom dancers
and I undo my thoughts
as I'm swept away
by natures melody

'She holds the moon close to her heart but keeps all the stars in her eyes'

~ Create Your Own Sunshine ~

Don't keep your authentic
expressions censored
You'll shine like the sun when
you are heart-centred
The more you are in your heart
You will express yourself at your highest
Whether creating or loving
It's there you'll be shining the brightest

*'And even with all the darkness her heart has known
She has a spirit like the sun.'*

~ Cascading Passion ~

My mouth could caress a hundred pairs of lips
But know which kiss was yours
I could get lost inside your eyes
So much depth, they have no need for shores
Behind your ocean eyes, I feel the heat of your heart, cascading passion flowing deep
And the warmth of your hands cupping my soul
As you love me to sleep

'My lips have cravings full of your kiss.'

~ Tiny Soldiers ~

Tiny soldiers in my heart
guard every breath I take
They keep rhythm in the battlefields
left behind from each mistake
Mostly they just build up walls
and rarely go to war
though when they merge with hope, inside my mind
they forget what they've been fighting for
I know there is an army in my heart
as sure as the sky's home to the stars
But when they fight against each other
My soul starts bleeding through their scars

*'Don't live in the past, you've already won those battles.
Use your scars as weapons, not as shackles.'*

~ Stardust ~

What if all the world is dreaming and I am not quite what I seem
I'm just a floating star who lights up another's dream
What if the moon was really Earth
shining from afar, crumbling into dust with every fluttering star
Then while all the world is sleeping, song-less birds learn how to sing
Every where now turned to stardust
Let us all again begin

'Earth is but a giant floating womb
Life is a labour of love
And maybe when we all leave this world
We are born to heavens beauty up above'

~ Balancing Dualism ~

Wherever is fire
There will be ash
Still waters will
Have known
A splash
Where there's
A rose
Will be a thorn
It's through the
Darkness that
Light is born
Where there's a
Soul that
Never sleeps
You'll find
A heart
That surely weeps
Through passion
May come many talents
The secret lies
In how you balance

*'It doesn't matter If you go out
with a bang or a whisper
Just don't become an echo
In between'*

~ Hungry Heart ~

I think you dipped me
in your essence
Left me fragranced
with your scent
My heart's been flavoured
with your presence
Much to
my minds torment

*'I never knew how hungry my heart was
Until I had a taste of your love'*

~ Hurricane Heart ~

She tries to calm
the storm within
But she's a hurricane
wrapped up with skin
There's thunder
crashing through her mind
And her lightning looks
will leave you blind

'She was heaven in a hurricane
Starlight within a storm'

~ The Magic of Children ~

When I look at my children
It's like seeing pieces
Of my soul
Little stars
shining bright
Making my universe whole
Roses
blossoming
Grown from the same garden
Breathing love
Ensuring this heart of mine
Will never harden

'Live your life
in such a way
that when your children
think of you
they'll remember
why they've always
believed in magic'

~ Lunar Soul ~

I think the moon
must be one big luminous soul
shining over all
to remind us of our connections
After all
It is the same moon we all see
wherever we may be
in the entire universe

*'Maybe the moon
is a different shape every night
Because it leaves little pieces
of its heart with us all'*

~ Scars ~

And scars
They stain
Like lesions
Deep within
Her soul and heart
But they gently
Fade through
Passing seasons
And she knows
How to wear them
Like art

*'When her heart was broken into a thousand stolen pieces,
She took hold of their sharp edges and sculptured herself
a thousand reasons to love some more'*

~ Heart Song ~

He hit me like a storm
though he is calmness epitomised
I swear that I could watch
the sunrise in his eyes
I can still feel the heat
from each of his kisses
My skin seems to know
It's his lips that it misses
He turns my sadness into music
But all too soon he is gone
I'll wait for his return
Because he's now
My favourite song

*'Some of my most favourite songs
are played in the sound of your heartbeat'*

~ The Beauty You See In Me Is A Reflection of What's Beautiful In You ~

I fall in love
a little bit more
every moment
of each day
With thoughts
and dreams
hopes and visions
words I want to say
I love the tiny simple things
Refreshing little sips
of sensations and feelings
laughter kissing
my soft lips
Most of all
I think I fall
for things my heart can see
The rawness inside my soul
The woman Within me

'I no longer wish for my dreams to come true, I gave myself the wings needed to go chase them.'

~ Redefining Romance ~

He entered her world like an arrow
Piercing her very core
Leaving her breathless
Craving, longing for more
More of his warm breath on her body
Besides the taste of his lips
She needed to feel his fire gently
Savouring sips
She had never before felt passion so fierce
Her heart and soul entered a trance
She was captivated by the enchantment
Exquisite lovers
Redefining romance

*'You kissed me so passionately with your eyes
Long before our lips ever met'*

~ Rainbows ~

When I found you
You thought
You were the dark
In need of light
But when
I touched you
I saw your colours
Shining bright
You just had to learn
How to make
Your colours show
Now you're
Bringing rainbows
Everywhere you go

*'But what if you don't struggle
with your darkness?
If you sit quietly and let it wrap itself around you for
long enough, maybe you'll get a glimpse of all the stars in
your heart.'*

~ Gypsy Soul ~

Make sure if you enter her aura
to keep your heart undercover
Her soul's unlike any before her
She'll stimulate you more than any lover
And I don't just mean the sensation
You'll feel all over your skin
When she gives you a glimpse of her mind
You will start melting within
The heat you feel between each of your bones
Like you're drowning in a sea
of pure Whiskey
Comes from the fire within
her own heart, beating wild,
For she has the soul of a gypsy

'She had a manifest charm
A proven ability
To live her own truth
And love unconditionally'

~ Happily Ever After ~

Shooting stars, making wishes
Long hugs, passionate kisses
Sunshine, flowers, big oak trees
Ocean shores, a summer breeze
Butterflies, mermaids, moonlight
Laying on the grass, on a starry night
Lions, tigers, wolves, giraffes
Seashells, kindness, babies laughs
Bubbles, champagne, lipstick
Giggling, singing, music
Memories, friends, family
Driving, art, history
Love, smiles, my children's laughter
These are my happy ever after

'Fall in love with sunsets, dance with the flowers. Tell secrets to the trees and never count the hours'

~ Soul Mate ~

I will forever be in love with him
and always be in lust
He'll feed fire and passion to my hungry heart
'Till my bones have turned to dust
Then I'll float into the velvet sky
Until night and I become whole
And I'll wait for him to join me
Stardust to dusty soul

*'When it's time to leave this life and move on to the next
I'll continue loving you
It's your soul mine likes the best'*

~ SoulFire ~

They will take many
things from me
at times even my dignity
Some gave me sorrow
some gave me blame
a few even handed me some shame
I've felt loss and painful goodbyes
but they've never taken the stars from my eyes
Some tried to tear me all apart
but I still have passion in my heart
And no one could ever again
make me feel less than whole
'Cause I'll keep the fire
In my soul

'Don't cut yourself on pieces of painful memories, take hold of their jagged tips and carve a path straight to your dreams'

~ Wings of A Storm ~

There was a storm
Inside of her
That raged
From time to time
A mountain stood
Inside her mind
That she didn't want
To climb
Sometimes at night
When sleep wouldn't come
She let the storm break
Until she was
Feeling numb
She then took a walk
Where angels
Fear to tread
She danced
With her demons
Around that mountain
And faced her fears instead

'Sometimes you'll find your inner peace on the wings of a storm'

~ Sensitive Souls ~

Some of the most sensitive ones I know, are free-spirited and seem to glow
But they sparkle because they care so much, feeling things they just can't touch
Sensing others moods and soaking up emotions, sometimes frustrations, even devotions.
Feeling the worlds pain becomes overwhelming and people can be overbearing
So our sensitive souls like to have secret places
To be alone and restore in quiet spaces

'Some can touch without feeling anything
And some feel everything with the absence of touch'

~ Butterflies ~

The wild hearts
never put boundaries
on their dreams
and aspirations
They follow
the winds of change
with hope
Creating inspiration
They'll allow
their wings to grow
So their souls
can soar and fly
Understanding that
transformation is needed
For a caterpillar
to become
a butterfly

'She has a rebel soul
Lives by her own state of anarchy
You see wild hearts can't be broken
And you can't tame what's meant to be free'

~ Shadow Keeper ~

As you lay thee
down to sleep
I'll whisper you
a dream to keep
Dreams of love
wrapping your heart tight
so you'll be safe
all through the night
The moon sings a lullaby
of hope and wishes
as shooting stars
sprinkle your soul
with kisses
And if the monsters
come out to play
I will send them
on their way
I'll be your dream catcher
your shadow keeper
so you can sleep
a little deeper
But if nightmarish demons
haunt you
when awake
I'll pray the angels
their souls to take

'Sometimes I keep my dreams, they make me feel safe. But nightmares are dreaming too, the worse kind when I'm awake.'

~ Kissing Cannibals ~

She danced with delusion
went frolicking with fear
she didn't allow her mind
to let things not there appear
she could venture with a vampire
or kiss a cannibal
she could fly so very high because she wasn't afraid to fall
she was right here in each moment, that she was alive
you could call it a defence mechanism, how she's learnt to survive
She won't try to see into the future
She shook away yesterday's dust
She's mindful in her mindfulness
She won't confuse love with lust
She's used all the prettiest colours to cover up her scars
She daydreams through the night
or you'll find her kissing stars
She believes that fear isn't real, it exists only in her thoughts
She chooses not to worry about what lies ahead
But she'll be afraid of something dangerous, of course
Imagination and anxiety build the fears of past hurts and pain
so she uses hers to find happiness, for benefits and gain
And she finds magic in each present moment
her memory keeps the ones she likes the most
Because the future is uncertain
And the past is just a ghost

'Somewhere at the edge of time she lost herself for a while, but on her way to forever she put her broken pieces back together'

~ Dance ~

My Soul is made
from music
My heart
drums the beat
Each day
I write lyrics
Some bitter
most sweet
I sing stories
of passion
Tales of
romance
Wherever life
leads me
I'll be sure
to dance

'My heart must be made of music
For I wouldn't be able to breathe
Without that beat'

~ Permanent Daylight ~

Some are pretty and with innocence comes beauty, but there's a quality of radiance I've seen that's rare

Some only shine so bright, if they've learnt to fight, either themselves or a deeper darkness somewhere

These people pave the way for others, some might save friends or lovers, they use their tragedies to inspire

With souls of luminance, hearts creating coalescence, they spread inspiration rapidly, like wildfire

And though they may find, the darkness creeps into their mind, enveloping thoughts turn black as night

Tackling delusion, shifting blame, learning to share they become illuminant, like moths drawn to a flame, lost souls everywhere ....

Become free to find their permanent daylight

'Those who shine from within will never be afraid of the dark'

~ Sea of Hopes & Dreams ~

The inside
of my eyelids
belong to another
time and place
And when
I close my eyes
and drift
quietly into space
I'm floating
in a flying boat
upon magical seas
Where thoughts
will never
let me drown
In oceans
of hopes and dreams

'It's easy to drown in your own thoughts, don't always believe everything you think'

~ Sleepless Memories ~

I want to erase you
from my mind
My mouth wants to forget
the taste of your kiss

I never again want my thoughts to find
how it feels divine
when I'm wrapped
in your arms like this

My skin doesn't want to
remember the tingles
It gets when
in contact with yours

Make my tummy
lose all memory
of the butterflies you send me
When my head thinks how perfect are all your flaws

My lips won't miss
kissing you
My body won't be missing you
My soul will still seek out yours to connect

Go ahead erase my mind
but I know you will find
yourself there in my heart
Which will never forget

'It's time to free the butterflies you once gave me'

~ Diamonds & Pearls ~

The only jewels
needed for
a girl like me
drops of moonlight
upon the sea
the diamonds
in your eyes
every time
you look at me
Or whispered
Pearls of poetry

*'But darling,
you are the pearl'*

~ Fairytale Charm ~

Some have a charm
of golden thread
they sew
throughout your heart
A tongue
dipped in silver
speaking pretty words
like art
Charismatic aura
enveloping your soul
like a gentle hug
from every
fairytale
Ever to be told

'I tasted his silver words dripping from his lips
They made for the most passionate, eloquent kiss'

~ Her Own Kind of Divinity ~

She is a goddess
a warrior
worth more than
her weight in gold
She is a guardian
a nurturer
With spirit young
and soul of old
She has words
for all occasions
and is wise
beyond her years
She has a heart
as big as oceans
and will always
face her fears

'Warrior woman, gentle, yet strong. Dances to the rhythm of her souls song. Playful heart, inner child, lives simply, heart full of wild.'

~ She Is You ~

She is heaven
in a hurricane
The shining explosion
of a shooting star
The melody
in the music
that you hear
echoing afar
She is the stirring
in your soul
The strong wind
and gentle breeze
She is the velvet petals
of every flower
The roots and branches
of all the trees
She is the glitch
in every lie
She is everything
that's true
She is a creation
of primitive art
I think she could be YOU

'It's like dust from a distant star showered through her every scar'

~ Rhythm of Life ~

She moves
rhythmically
through life
with grace
and endurance
Making choices
with patience
and acceptance
Always
staying true
to herself
She is able
to embrace
the fallout
of her decisions
with non-judgement
Then continue
her journey
With love in her heart

'Chaos sometimes collided with her soul but her mind knew when to let it go. And though her heart felt heavy from the hurt, she was a warrior woman who knew her worth'

~ Realm of Romance ~

She was a paradox
of simplicity and chaos
pleasing to the senses
and mind aesthetically
She was light and delicate
in a way that seemed
too perfect for this world
And I think that's why
she created her own
a realm full
of romantic possibilities

'She lives in fairy tales of imagined dreams
Where she's protected from the twisted truth and forbidden love
of forgotten memories'

~ Majestic Grace ~

She had a love affair
with trees
heard each gentle sigh
with every falling leaf
and danced along
with their branches
when they frolicked
in the breeze
She marvelled
at their ever
majestic grace
an elegance not found
upon a persons face
She had an understanding
that each one
had its own soul
welcoming new growth
while staying true
to deep roots
Evergreen
yet remaining whole

'Allow yourself to listen to the whispering wisdom of nature's wildness, and she will carry you to the raw wild inside your own heart'

~ Footprints ~

You may never get
to place your lips
upon my very own
But I feel their warmth
in all the space
between my every bone
Though you might
not feel the contours
and curve of my full hips
It's almost like
they're on reserve
for the touch of your fingertips
And all the pieces of our hearts
may not get the chance
to become whole
But I know
our heartbeats
dance together
Because they
left footprints
Deep inside my soul

*'Regret echoes down the path not chosen
From inside a heart behind a door never to be opened'*

~ Silken Threads ~

If her soul was fashioned into clothing
For all the world to see
It would be the colours of Springtime
With silken threads all shimmery
Flowering blossoms could be seen
Trailing along the part
Where it stays evergreen
From all the love inside her heart
And when she looked into the mirror
To see how she reflects
She'd see love
Patience and kindness
Stitched together as a dress

'She was simply magic and she made being magical look simple'

~ Rare Gem ~

She's not diamonds and pearls
Silver or gold
She's more precious than crystals
You'll ever hold
She's worth more than any treasure
You could hope to find
She's a gem unlike any
Jewellery shop kind

'She is so much more than it would seem, she is the Jewel inside a dream. Her attitude on life is quite contagious, always happy and vivacious. So reality aligns itself with her, to give the best that it can offer'

~ Alpha ~

~ Me ~
Passionate
Intense
Feeling
Using every sense
Each emotion
Every day
Felt devotion
Want to play
Craving affection
Hold me close
Need protection
Bleeding rose

~ He ~
Calm within my storm
Soothing touch
Caressing my soul
Serenity much
Kisses sweet
Let me fly
lips meet
Kissing third eye
Leader of the pack
Make me yield
Steal me away
Forever my shield

'She dances with Wolves to the rhythm of her heartbeat'

~ Pokerface ~

His eyes made oceans seem tiny in comparison
I could drown in their depths
Or dance along with their passion
But when he was sad they were almost transparent
Absorbing everything in view
Making him seem absent
There was starfire in those eyes
He was worlds apart
He was a warrior of battles
That left scars inside his heart
He could touch me tenderly
Even with his strength of each hand
He made love to my mind
And put the 'gentle'
Into gentleman

'I see the hell in your heart and raise you the heaven in mine'

~ Crown ~

When it's time
for her to lay down
at the end of the day
Her mind puts to rest
all the words
that they say
She knows
in her heart
what is true for her
She'll only listen
to her own soul
and spirit whisper
She has
no need
for pretence
She is her
own form
of royalty
And she wears a crown
made of truth,
pride and loyalty

'A woman who knows her worth knows she never needs to prove it'

~ Sea of Love ~

They say there's plenty
Of fish in the sea
But I'm no fisherman
And will never be
I like things to flow
Such as rivers and streams
With different channels
Reaching for their dreams
But brooks and ponds
Are no good you see
For my heart is for him
He's the ocean to me

'If roses grew in places new each time he crossed my mind
A floral never-ending sea everywhere you'd find'

~ Empathy ~

Her sensitive soul sometimes wants to float away in a bubble
where nothing can touch her

Some days everything can hurt
even her own hair hurts her head but she lets the pain empower

She'll use depths of emotion with its sharpened edges to carve
a path to wisdom within

Becoming stronger from her sensitivities despite overwhelming
sensations she feels upon her velvet skin

Empathy flows through her veins then compassion breeds
from there

With an ability to heal
she will show others
how to care

She believes in fighting for what's right for her soul hurts if met
with unfairness

She is strength at its highest power layered with beautiful
gentleness

*'Then her breathless heart tore in two, became a pair of wings and
away she flew'*

~ Make Love To My Mind ~

Caress my cognisance
Stroke my intellect
Show me your genius
Give me a climax I won't forget
Taste my pearl of wisdom
When you go down on my mind
Plant kisses on my perception
Leave my senses blind
Touch me in the places
You can't reach with fingertips
Make love to my imagination
I'll kiss your thoughts
without using my lips

*'And there you go again
Caressing all my senses'*

~ Sips of Stars ~

Fragments of my heart
were lost along
the way somewhere
But when I looked
into your eyes
I found the missing
pieces there
The moment
you first kissed me
felt like tasting
stars in little sips
I knew then
that I'd found home
With my lips
against your lips

'Whenever my soul is feeling lost and my heart stumbles and trips, I find my way home by the trail of stardust, your kiss left upon my lips'

~ Forget-Me-Not ~

It was as if she left a trail of flowers with her beauty, wherever she would go. Her soul blossomed from within, Yet she didn't know. A fragranced blanket of her sweet scent
wrapped around all that she went near, she was like a soft opaque light, and wistful whisperings of cheer. But even though she shines brighter than any star, no one thought to let her know, they admired from afar. Her words although powerful, were softly spoken,
resembling gentle ringing chimes, but no one told her she is beautiful ...

And she forgets sometimes.

'Make her feel flowers bloom in all the places you touch her, but don't forget to touch her heart.'

~ Inner Child ~

Sometimes she was
a mermaid
Swam on
the oceans shore
Sometimes she was
Oliver Twist
Not afraid
to ask for more
When she was
a ballerina
She'd point her toes
and twirl
She'll forever
be a lady
And always
a little girl

'Always stand up for what you believe in, but forever let the wonder and magic of life bring you to your knees'

~ Stain ~

You leave a stain on society
A bitter taste in the world
You might be different in sobriety
Guess that flag won't be unfurled
I wonder how you feel
When you've left her feeling numb
Sure, her bruising will heal
But she'll stay underneath your thumb
You prey on her kind
Believing she is weak
You know others will act blind
And turn the other cheek
I hope one day she'll realise
That she can be so strong
She'll stop listening to your lies
And you'll end up where you belong

'Then one day hope reached into her chest, grabbed hold of her heart and called
Come fly with me'

~ Independent Woman ~

She shared her heart with many
For it was filled with so much love
She loved so many things in life
Like sunshine, rain and stars above
Her soul was not reliant
She did not need to depend
Reassurance wasn't necessary
Her heart was her souls friend
She enjoyed another's company
But wasn't afraid to be on her own
Once she found peace within herself
She was never lonely, when she was alone

'There's a sensual longing inside of her to find a mind of intellectual quality. Her soul will look for another of depth to stimulate her development of consciousness, her gentle heart will change its rhythm when close to other sensitive hearts that keep something wild within them'.

~ Infinite Potential ~

Inside each and every one of us
Is an infinite potential we should trust
Our inner strength you must believe
of unlimited capacity to achieve
Being strong is not about what you can do
It's all about what you've been through
Overcoming things you thought you wouldn't
Making a could out of a couldn't
And remember part of being strong
Is knowing you don't always have to be
True strength is in us all along
Just open your heart
And set it free

'Time will never stop some feelings, or take the pain away, it's in the stillness of remembering we learn to cope some more each day.'

~ Perpetual Princess ~

She sits inside my mind
Always patient, forever kind
Murmuring notions of poetic beauty
She helps my heart see things
Makes thoughts fly with whispering wings
She is my perpetual princess of poetry
When I free my hair, from the ribbons that I wear
And my soft tendrils fall about my face
She has me believe it's raining petals and leaves
And the moment has me drifting out to space
Sometimes she gets sad but seldom she is mad
Her light may dim and flicker for a little while
Those times remind me of tangible dualities
Would we recognise kindness without any cruelties?
If there was no dark, we wouldn't see light spark
And she always seems to know how to make my soul smile

'She walks with beauty but her tears tell their own story, her heart hides scars, but her mind is a princess of poetry'

~ FireStone ~

Yes, her heart
was a little tattered
Her soul
just slightly bruised
But her mind
was a gorgeous
mess of chaos
and all the thoughts
she mused
You see her heart
was filled
with so much love
despite what
they had took
And her soul
was strong
as Firestone
She had a backbone
built entirely of characters
from each and every
favourite book

'For all the books that touched my heart and all the words that kissed my soul'

MICHELLE SCHAPER

~ Whiskey Angels with Wings of Ink ~

This goes out to those
With the flamed whiskey souls
Who feel passion burn
Through their blood, a yearn
The longing to be
Something wild and carefree
But they're caged in their thoughts
A prison of sorts
So for you they will bring
Spilled ink to sing
Their reflections of mind
Sometimes sad, mostly kind
Giving words a sweet cadence
Rhythmical decadence
Connecting through shared sorrows
Or dreaming of our tomorrows
Uniting us all
With each rise and fall
The dreamers, ones called 'a poet'
Softening the madness
of life as we know it

'If you can feel ink flowing through your veins, stirring echoes of light in each shadowed part, let it spill whispers of enchantment and free the beautiful wings fluttering inside your heart'

Printed in Great Britain
by Amazon